KAYTEE, QUEEN OF THE PIRATES

BY
TONY WHISNANT

ILLUSTRATED BY CHARLO NOCETE

To order additional copies of this book, contact:
Xlibris Corporation
1-888-795-4274
www.Xlibris.com
Orders@Xlibris.com

This book is dedicated to Mrs. Hagler and Mrs. Hagler's 2010-2011 Third Grade Class at Franklin Forest Elementary School, Troup County, Georgia. Had it not been for them, Kaytee and her adventure would have stayed hidden away in a treasure chest, buried deep in the imagination, never to be found.

"Oh, Kaytee, not again!" her mother scolded, exasperatedly. "How did you get your clothes dirty in such a short amount of time?"

"I'm a pirate, Mommy. Arrrrgggg!" was Kaytee's only explanation.

"I went to attack two ships. I took their treasure, and buried it in the sand over there," Kaytee said pointing toward the mound of dirt on the floor next to the potted plant Mrs. Markel had on the table by the window.

Kaytee's mother looked in the direction that Kaytee pointed. There beside the bookcase and next to the window was a pile of dirt — on the table, on the bookcase, on the freshly cleaned carpet. Mrs. Markel's mouth flew open, "Oh Kaytee!" was the only thing that Mrs. Markel was able to say.

"I buried it good, didn't I, Mommy?" Kaytee asked.

Mrs. Markel didn't know whether to clean up the mess first or walk out the door. "Oh Kaytee!" was all that she could say.

Mrs. Markel got a broom and dust pan, paper napkins, and a trash can. She got the mess up as best she could.

When Mrs. Markle looked down at the mess in the dustpan, she saw a box. It was the pen and pencil set that she and Kaytee bought Mr. Markel for his birthday. "Oh, Kaytee. You buried your father's gift."

"I know," said Kaytee, "I didn't want any other pirates to get it. It is my treasure now to give to my daddy."

"OK, Kaytee, let's go." When they started out the door Mrs. Markel still had the trash can in her hands. She took the trash can back into the house and came back out. "Mommy, are we leaving now?" asked Kaytee.

"Why, yes, Kaytee, we have to go to get groceries." She stopped suddenly in her tracks. She had forgotten baby Rodney.

Finally, in the car, they started to the grocery store.

When they arrived, Mrs. Markel took Kaytee and Baby Rodney out of their car seats. Mrs. Markel was glad when they arrived and she could put Kaytee in the buggy. Mrs. Markel put Baby Rodney in the front of the cart and Kaytee got in the shopping part of the cart.

"Kaytee, I want you to stay seated in the basket while we shop. If you get up, you could fall out and you could hurt yourself badly."

"Ok, Mommy," was Kaytee's only reply with such an angelic smile that Mrs. Markel's heart melted. "Oh, Kaytee, I love you so much."

Mrs. Markel picked up a big pack of paper towels and laid them on Kaytee. Kaytee was hidden by the paper towels. Kaytee remained in the basket until the cart was parked and another cart parked next to them in the cereal aisle.

Mrs. Markel turned her back to pick up some cereal. Another child about Kaytee's age was in the other buggy. He was covered by a blanket which he removed when the buggy stopped.

Kaytee looked at the boy, the boy looked at Kaytee. Kaytee said, "Hey, I am Kaytee, Queen of the Pirates. Arrrrgggg!"

"I am Jeffy," said the boy, "I am a ghost. Boo!" .

Mrs. Markel and Jeffy's mom crossed paths looking for their cereals.

They smiled at each other and stepped out of each other's way.

"**M**ove over," said Kaytee, "I am coming aboard your ship, I am pirating it." Out of the buggy came Kaytee. She got in the buggy with Jeffy and Kaytee threw the blanket over both of them.

The paper towels that had hidden Kaytee were in the basket, Jeffy was there in his basket, and the buggies were still in the same places.

Mrs. Markel came back to her buggy suspecting nothing wrong. Jeffy's mom came back to her buggy. The two ladies again smiled and greeted each other. They never suspected that Jeffy's mom carried a stowaway. Mrs. Markel and Jeffy's mom went their separate ways.

Jeffy's mom could hear Jeffy ask questions and she would answer.

"Are you really a pirate?" Jeffy asked Kaytee.

But Jeffy's mom thought he was talking to her.

"No silly, I am your mom," said Jeffy's mom.

Jeffy and Kaytee laughed.

Jeffy's mom was bent over the canned goods and did not hear Jeffy and Kaytee laugh. Jeffy's mom placed the cans in the basket and started off. Kaytee got off balanced and fell backward.

At the same time, Mrs. Markel was still shopping and keeping one eye on Baby Rodney and one eye on Kaytee- or so she thought. She stopped at the bread aisle and asked Kaytee if she wanted some donuts. When Kaytee did not answer, Mrs. Markel lifted the paper towel pack.

Kaytee was no where in the basket. She was not under the basket. Kaytee was not beside her. Kaytee was not behind her. Mrs. Markel began to panic.

Across the store, Mrs. Markel heard a woman scream. "This is not my child!" yelled the woman. Mrs. Markel knew where to look.

Jeffy's mom began running. Mrs. Markel began running.

Jeffy's mom went up one aisle. Mrs. Markel went down another.

Jeffy's mom went past the beans, the potatoes, the rice. Mrs. Markel went past the meats, the cheeses, the fruits.

Jeffy's mom passed the breakfast pastries, the sugar, the fruit-flavored gelatins. Mrs. Markel rushed past the cookies, the crackers, the jellies.

Mrs. Markel stopped.

Mrs. Markel heard Kaytee laughing and she heard another child laughing.

Mrs. Markel was close.

Again, Mrs. Markel heard the lady scream, "This is not my child! Help!"

Mrs. Markel turned her buggy around and ran up the aisle she had come down.

There was the lady with the stowaway child. The lady was frantic. Mrs. Markel had been frantic, too. Mrs. Markel slowed the frightened lady down. The lady looked at Mrs. Markel. Mrs. Markel looked at the lady. They remembered seeing each other on the cereal aisle.

To Mrs. Markel, Jeffy said, "Hi! My name is Jeffy. I am a ghost."

"I am glad to meet you, Jeffy. I am Mrs. Markel. I think you are a fine young man instead of a ghost," said Mrs. Markel.

Kaytee, not to be out done, introduced herself to Jeffy's mom, " I am Kaytee, Queen of the Pirates. Arrrrgggg! I pirated Jeffy's ship."

"And almost scared the 'Arrrrgggg' out of me. I am glad to know who you are Kaytee. I am Mrs. James."

To Mrs. Markel, Mrs. James said, "Call me Jenny." Mrs. Markel said, "I am Alice. After this adventurous trip to the store this morning, we need to go for a large chocolate donut."

"I will go for that," said Mrs. James, "and I'm buying!"

And that is just what they did as soon as the groceries were paid for and Kaytee was given back to her mother.

Made in the USA
San Bernardino, CA
12 December 2013